A verbal and visual feast, as well as an introduction to a rich indigenous culture, **Fire Race** will keep readers on the edge of their seats.

"It will take a lot of searching to find a more beautifully illustrated or carefully researched adaptation than this retelling of the Karuk tale of how fire came to the people."
—*American Bookseller*, Pick of the Lists

". . .sure-fire appeal for even the wiggliest of story-hour listeners."
—*School Library Journal*

"A beautiful combination of text and pictures. . ."
—*Booklist*

"This spirited Native American legend is in good hands."
—*Publishers Weekly*

Winner of the Society of Illustrators Award and Bookbuilder's West Award

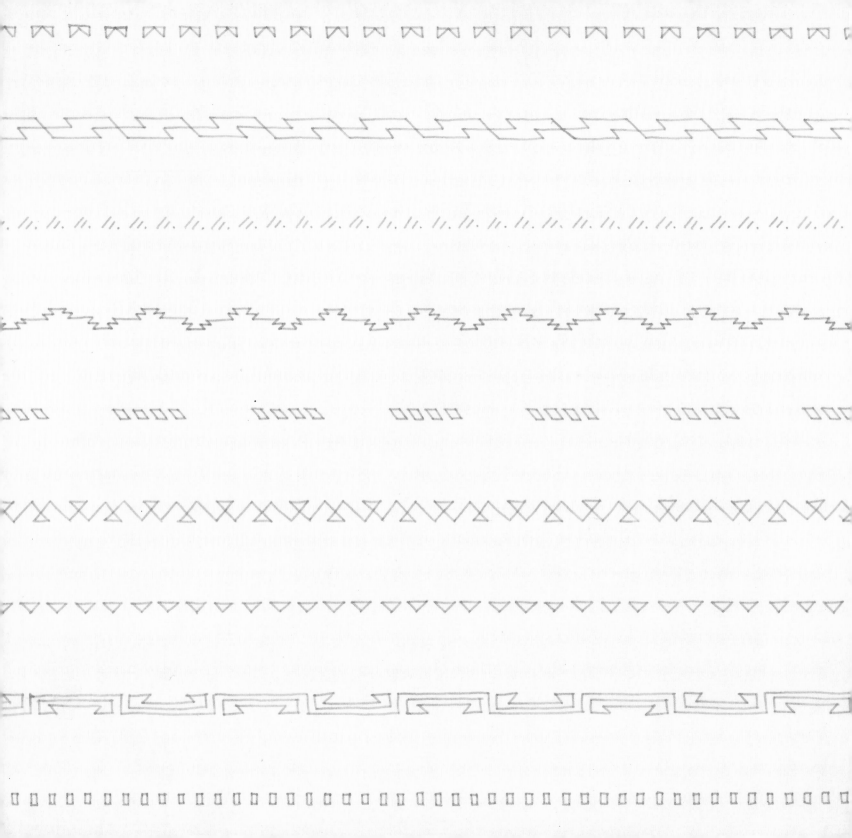

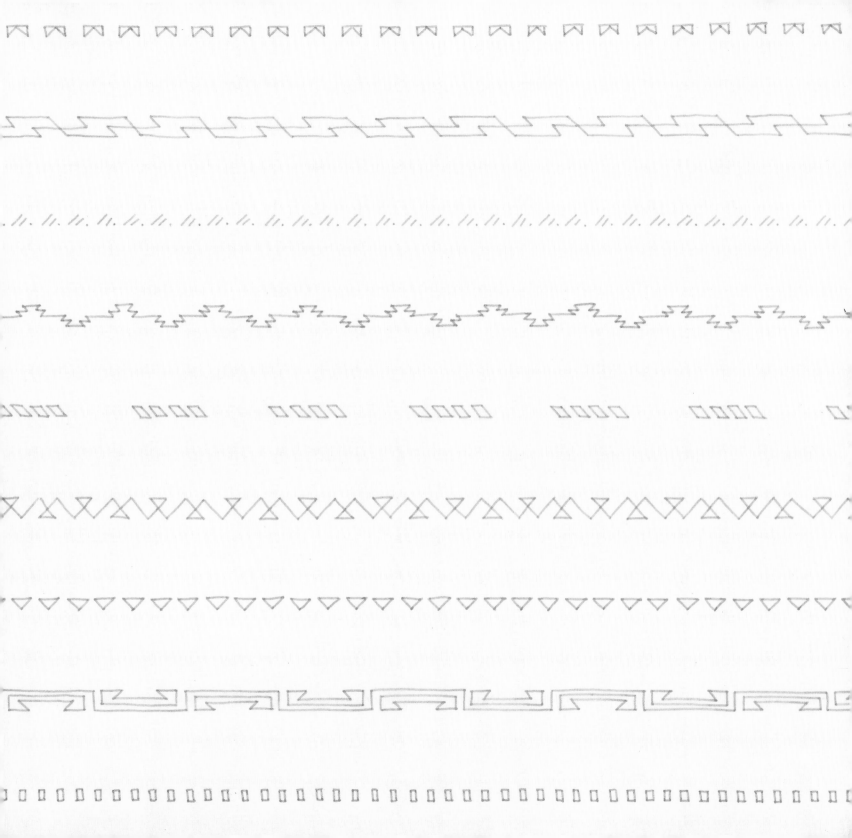

Author's Note:

This story is based on various versions of the Karuk myth. The Karuk—meaning "upriver"—people are native to the rugged Klamath River region of Northwest California. With their neighbors the Yurok, Hupa, and Shasta, they share many of the old stories. This is one.

Text copyright © 1993 by Jonathan London.
Illustrations copyright © 1993 by Sylvia Long.
Afterword copyright © 1993 by Julian Lang.

Book design by Alison K. Berry.
Manufactured in Singapore.

Library of Congress Cataloging-in-Publication Data
London, Jonathan, 1947-
Fire Race: a Karuk coyote tale about how fire came
to the people / by Jonathan London and Lanny
Pinola; with an afterword by Julian Lang; illustrated
by Sylvia Long.
Summary: With the help of other animals,
Wise Old Coyote manages to acquire fire from
the wicked Yellow Jacket sisters.
ISBN 0-8118-1488-2 (pb) 0-8118-0241-8 (hc)
1. Karuk Indians–Legends. 2. Coyote (Legendary
Character)–Legends. 3.Fire–Folklore. [1. Karuk
Indians–Legends. 2. Indians of North
America–California–Legends. 3. Fire–Folklore.
4. Coyote (Legendary Character)]
I. Pinola, Lanny. II. Long, Sylvia, ill. III. Title.
E99.k25L65 1993   92-32352
398.24'52974442–dc20   CIP
                                AC

Distributed in Canada by Raincoast Books
9050 Shaughnessy Street, Vancouver, British Columbia V6P 6E5

10 9 8 7 6 5

Chronicle Books LLC
85 Second Street
San Francisco, California 94105

www.chroniclekids.com

To the People who loved these stories, made them come alive, and passed them on.

With thanks to Ricardo Sierra, from whom I first heard a version of this story; to Sue Plummer, Sebastopol's children's librarian; to Joe Bruchac, Abenaki storyteller; and to Linda Vit, Karuk artist.
—*Jonathan London*

For my parents with love and thanks for their wisdom, encouragement and kindness. Their joy in each other and the natural world around them is a continuing source of pleasure and inspiration for their children.
—*Sylvia Long*

To my grandmother, Elizabeth Conrad, who first told me this story and many more; to Jubilee, my son, and to Lisa.
—*Julian Lang*

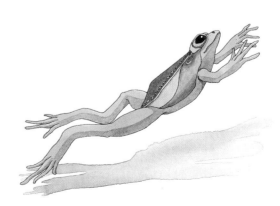

FIRE RACE

A Karuk Coyote Tale About How Fire Came to the People

retold by Jonathan London with Lanny Pinola
illustrated by Sylvia Long
with an afterword by Julian Lang

chronicle books · san francisco

Long ago, the animal people had no fire. Day and night, they huddled in their houses in the dark, and ate their food uncooked. In the winter, they were so cold, icicles hung from their fur. Oh, they were miserable!

Then one day, Wise Old Coyote gathered everybody together. "We have heard about fire," he said. "But the only fire is far upriver, at the world's end. It's guarded by the Yellow Jacket sisters high atop a snowy mountain. They are wicked, and will not share it. But listen, if we all cooperate and work together, we can steal the fire." There was much fearful murmuring about the Yellow Jacket sisters, but all grew quiet as Coyote told them his plan. Then he went on his way.

Grandfather Coyote slowly trudged up the mountain at the world's end.
When at last he came to the Yellow Jacket's house, smoke was rising
from the smokehole.

Coyote looked inside. The three old sisters were sitting around the fire.
Coyote said, as friendly as can be, "If you let me in, I'll make you all look pretty."
Suspicious, the three sisters put their heads close together and buzzed.
"Come in," they said. "But no tricks!"

Old Man Coyote sat down and took a chunk of oak bark between his toes and held it in the fire. When it had burned into a blackened coal, he marked their yellow faces and bodies with black stripes to make them pretty. "Now," said Coyote, "if you close your eyes, I will make you even prettier."

Here was Coyote's chance! While the Yellow Jackets' eyes were closed, he took the charred oak in his teeth, and silent as the moon in the sky, he crept outside. Then he raced down the mountain like the wind.

When the Yellow Jacket sisters found out that Coyote had tricked them, they were screaming mad. They, too, flew like the wind. And it wasn't long until they caught up to Coyote.

They were almost on him when Coyote tripped, rolled downhill like a snowball, and landed smack at Eagle's feet. Snatching the glowing coal in his talons, Eagle spread his wings and took to the sky.

Eagle was swift, but the Yellow Jackets soon caught up with him. Suddenly, Eagle dropped the coal. Below, Mountain Lion caught it in his great teeth, and bounded off through the snow. Still, the furious Yellow Jackets followed.

Just as they were about to sting Mountain Lion, Fox snatched the fiery coal, and bounced in among the tall cedar and pine. Fox ran and ran, until she was so tired, she couldn't take another step. She huffed and huffed. Her breath made clouds, and the Yellow Jackets were right behind her.

Just in time, Bear took the fire and lunged away through some brambles.

Bear, too, was quick, yet the Yellow Jackets were right on top of her.

Even Bear could not fight them off, and she finally tumbled in exhaustion.

As Bear fell, Measuring Worm, the Long One, took the fire. The Long One stretched way out over three ridges, yet the Yellow Jackets were there, waiting, ready to strike.

Somehow, right under the Yellow Jackets's eyes, Turtle sneaked in, grabbed the fire, and scrambled off. But of course Turtle was slow, and one of the Yellow Jacket sisters stung him in his tail. *Akee! Akee! Akee!*

Turtle pulled in his head and legs and flip-flopped down the hill. *Fallumph.*
Fallumph. Fallumph. The Yellow Jackets were swarming all over Turtle, when
Frog leaped out of the river and swallowed the fire. *Gulp!*

Then Frog hopped back into the river – *plop* – and sat on the bottom. The Yellow Jackets stormed the river, circling once, circling twice, circling three times, buzzing the surface. They waited and they waited and they waited, but Frog held the fire, and his breath. Finally, the Yellow Jackets gave up, and flew back home.

As soon as the Yellow Jacket sisters were gone, Frog burst out of the water, and spat the hot coal into the roots of a willow growing along the river. The tree swallowed the fire, and the animal people didn't know what to do.

Then once again Coyote came along, and the animal people said, "Grandfather, you must show us how to get the fire from the willow." So Old Man Coyote, who is very wise and knows these things, said, "Hah!" and he showed them how to rub two willow sticks together over dry moss to make fire.

From that time on the people have known how to coax fire from the wood in order to keep warm and to cook their food. And at night in the seasons of cold, they have sat in a circle around their fires and listened as the elders told the old stories. And so it is, even to this day. *Kupanakanakana.*

AFTERWORD

Ishpukatunvêech iikiv
a "little money" necklace

Storytelling is very important for the Karuk people. Both children and adults are taught through stories about the special relationship that we must keep between ourselves and the natural world. The Karuk people are Fix the Earth People. Many of us gather each year to clean special ceremonial places, to pray for water food and earth food. We pray so the children and elders will be healthy. We ask that the natural world around us become stable and remain balanced.

Traditional stories describe the natural world and human nature. In *Fire Race,* we are reminded just how important the willow tree is to our way of life. We are told of one way that Coyote helped us (he most often fooled people and caused great calamity). We are reminded that we must remember and respect each other. The story reveals that all natural living things are important, from the little frog to the soaring eagle.

Today, many Karuk children are told this story in their native language. Often stories contain ancient songs and funny jokes. Stories like *Fire Race* help the Karuk people love themselves. The stories are called *pikva* and are most often told during the winter months. During the spring, summer, and fall, we see all the animals and places that were spoken of in the stories. This, then, is wisdom from the Karuk people: the land, the people and the animals are all related.

Yootva!

– Julian Lang

BIBLIOGRAPHY

KAROK MYTHS by A.L. Kroeber and E.W. Gifford (University of California Press; most notably the stories told by Little Ike in 1902 and Mary Ike in 1940)

GIVING BIRTH TO THUNDER, SLEEPING WITH HIS DAUGHTER by Barry Lopez (Andrews & McNeel, Inc., 1977)

KARUK: THE UPRIVER PEOPLE by Maureen Bell (Naturegraph Publishers, 1991)

TO THE AMERICAN INDIAN: REMINISCENCES OF A YUROK WOMAN by Lucy Thompson (Heyday Books, 1991; original copyright 1916)

THE HOVER COLLECTION OF KARUK BASKETS by the Clarke Memorial Musuem/Eureka, California (1985)

DAWN OF THE WORLD: COAST MIWOK MYTHS by Hart Merrian, ed. by Bonni Peterson (1976)

THE MAIDU INDIAN MYTHS AND STORIES OF HANC'IBYJIM ed. and trans. by William Shipley (Heyday Books, 1991)

COYOTE WAS GOING THERE by Jerry Ramsey (Washington University Press, 1977)

THE EARTH IS OUR MOTHER: A GUIDE TO THE INDIANS OF CALIFORNIA by Dolan Eargle, Jr. (Tree's Company Press, 1986, 1991)

KEEPERS OF THE ANIMALS: NATIVE AMERICAN STORIES AND WILDLIFE ACTIVITIES FOR CHILDREN by Michael J. Caduto and Joseph Bruchac (Fulcrum, 1991)

Yuxchananach iikiv
abalone chip necklace

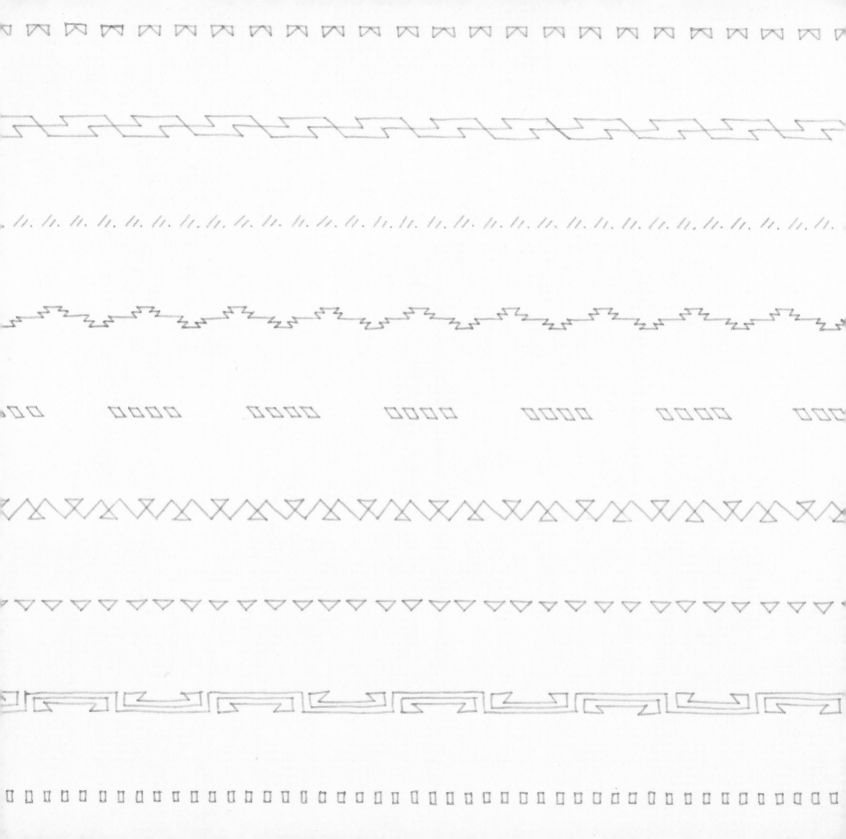

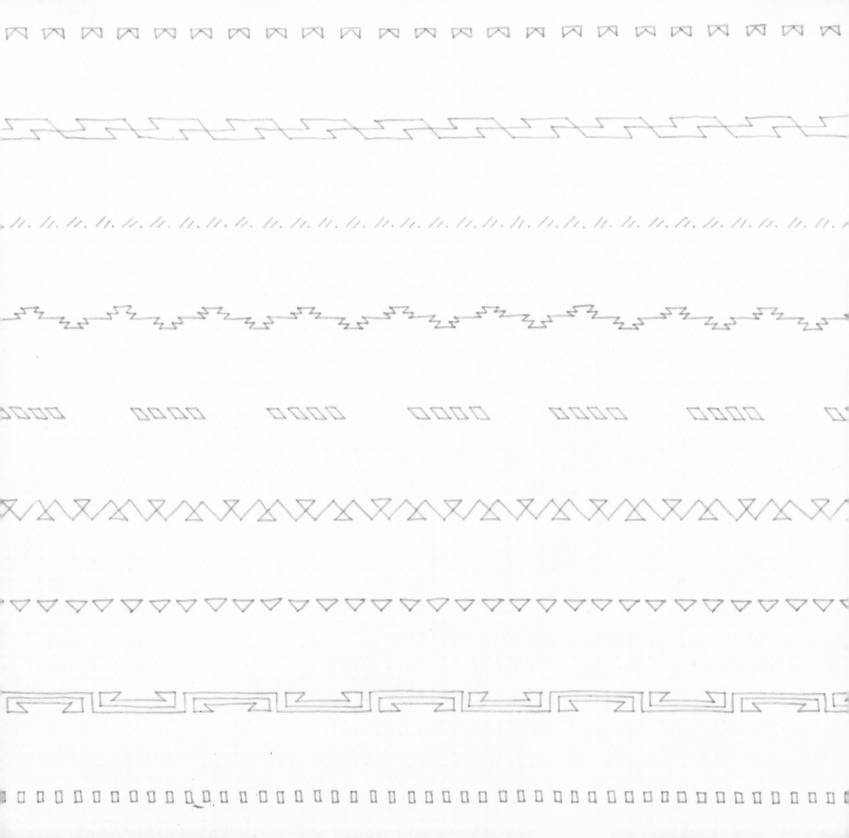

Jonathan London lives in Northern California with his wife and two sons. He has written many books for children. Mr. London's books reflect his love and respect for the natural world.

Sylvia Long is the illustrator of several books for children including the best-selling books *Hush Little Baby* and *Ten Little Rabbits*. Ms. Long's detail illustrations are inspired by her love of animals and the outdoors. She lives in Arizona with her husband and their two sons, Matthew and John.

Also written by Jonathan London:
Liplap's Wish, illustrated by Sylvia Long
Hip Cat, illustrated by Woodleigh Marx Hubbard
Fire Race, illustrated by Sylvia Long
Baby Whale's Journey, illustrated by Jon Van Zyle
The Eyes of the Gray Wolf, illustrated by Jon Van Zyle
Honey Paw and Lightfoot, illustrated by Jon Van Zyle

Also illustrated by Syliva Long:
Twinkle, Twinkle, Little Star, by Sylvia Long
Sylvia Long's Mother Goose, by Sylvia Long
Sylvia Long's Mother Goose Nesting Blocks, by Sylvia Long
Deck the Hall, by Sylvia Long
Hush Little Baby, by Sylvia Long
Ten Little Rabbits, by Virginia Grossman
Liplap's Wish, by Jonathan London
Alejandro's Gift, by Richard E. Albert